For my wonderful daughter, Lena;
to her fantastic dad, Gary;
and to my father, who taught me
to make my dreams come true

With special thanks to Laura for making
this book happen

Over the Moon

An Adoption Tale

Karen Katz

Henry Holt and Company   New York

Once upon a time a teeny-tiny baby was born.

That night a woman far away had a dream.
She dreamed she saw the baby in a basket surrounded
by beautiful violet flowers and birds of many colors.

Her husband dreamed of the same child.
He saw her beside the sea and mountains,
smiling a little smile, and he knew she was
the child they had been longing for.

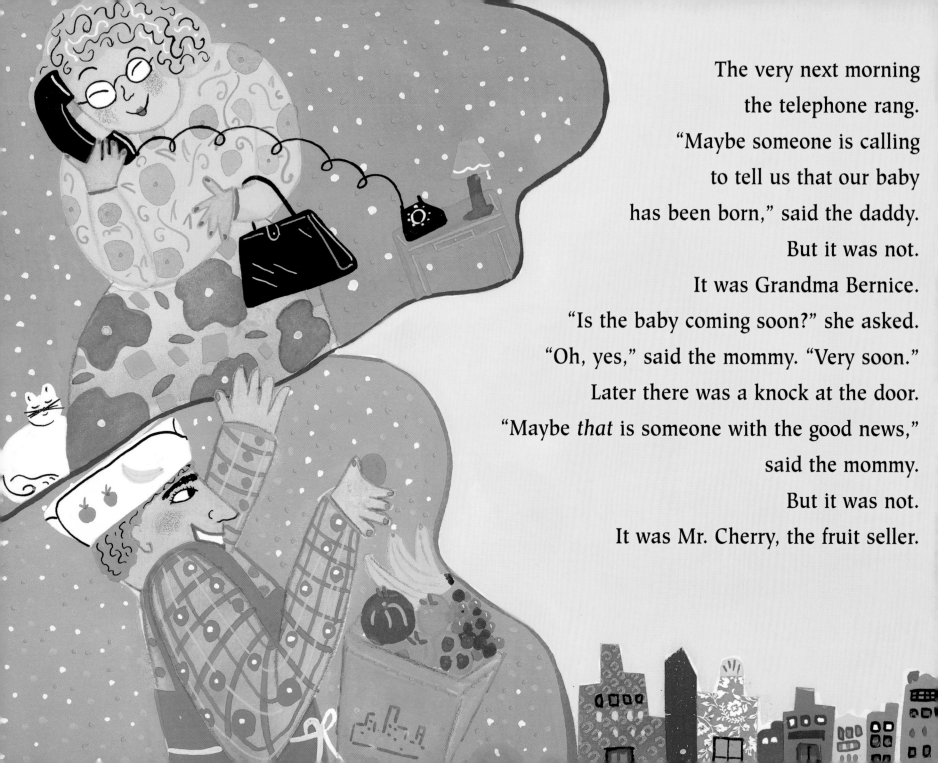

The very next morning
the telephone rang.
"Maybe someone is calling
to tell us that our baby
has been born," said the daddy.
But it was not.
It was Grandma Bernice.
"Is the baby coming soon?" she asked.
"Oh, yes," said the mommy. "Very soon."
Later there was a knock at the door.
"Maybe *that* is someone with the good news,"
said the mommy.
But it was not.
It was Mr. Cherry, the fruit seller.

"Is your baby coming soon?"
he asked.
"Everyone wants to know."
"Oh, yes," said the daddy.
"Very soon."
At dusk the sky turned blue and
darkness rolled over the city.
Molly, the little girl from next door,
peeked in the window.
"I can't wait to see the new baby!"
she said.
"Soon, soon," said the mommy
and daddy together.
"You will see the baby
very soon."

The moon came out. The stars twinkled.
And the telephone rang once more.

"Your baby has been born!
She is wonderful.
Come quickly and get her."

"At last!" they cried.

And they began to pack:

diapers
and stuffed bunnies,
little pink bottles
with funny nipples,
a stroller with green wheels,
pajamas of the softest cotton,
teeny-tiny T-shirts,
a shiny new rattle,
even a new baby blanket
with sparkles and lace.

Out the door they ran, into the car they jumped,
and off they drove to get their baby.
Quickly, quickly they sped over the bridge,
past the park, and to the airport.

There, they flew away on a giant airplane to a faraway place where their baby was waiting. Over the moon and through the night...

. . . until finally
they arrived and went
to a hotel to unpack.
Then they hurried
and scurried about,
getting the room ready
for their new baby.
"Soon, soon. Our baby
will be here soon,"
they told each other
as they waited.

Then through the window they saw her, carried

by the kind people who had taken care of her.

The door opened and there was the baby all soft and small.

At last she was in her new mommy's and daddy's arms.

Over the top of the blanket two tiny eyes looked up at them,

and the mommy and daddy looked back at her.

Then they hugged her and hugged her—at least a hundred times!

They were so happy.

Still, the new mommy
and daddy were nervous.
They had never taken care
of a teeny-tiny baby before.

and played with her

But they fed her

and changed her

and bathed her.

And before they knew it,
their first day as a family was over,
and they could not wait
for the next one to begin.

That night they took the baby
out to see the stars,
where they told her the story
of how she came to be
their little girl.
"You grew like a flower
in another lady's tummy
until you were born.
But the lady wasn't able
to take care of you, so
Mommy and Daddy came
to adopt you and
bring you home.
Even before you were born
we dreamed about you.
We knew we were
meant to be together."

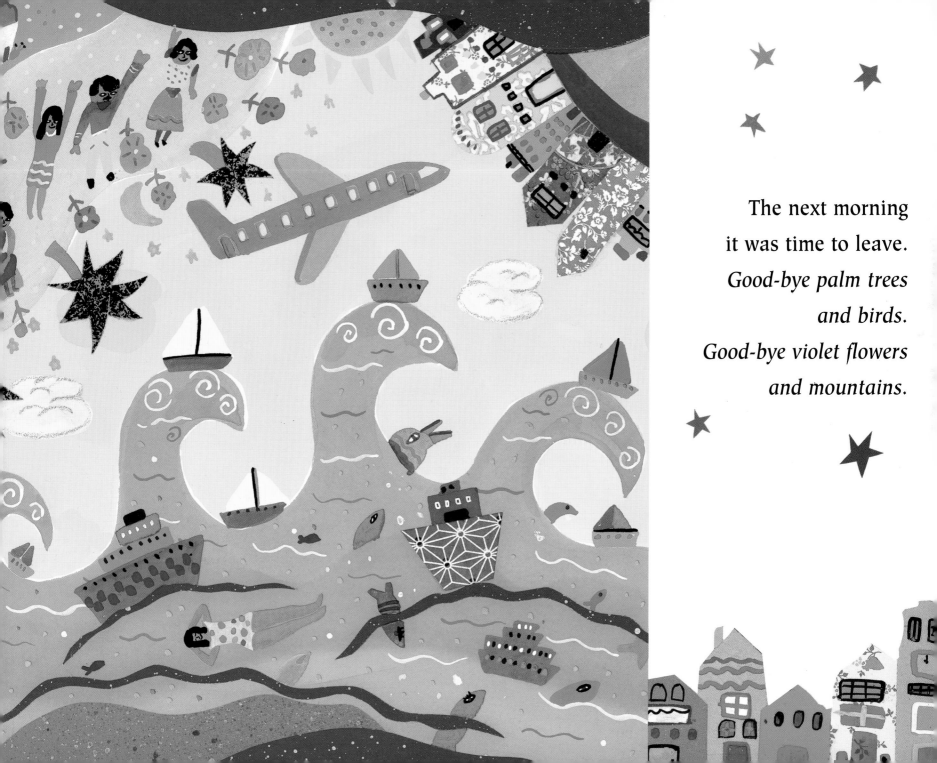

The next morning
it was time to leave.
*Good-bye palm trees
and birds.*
*Good-bye violet flowers
and mountains.*

Then they were HOME!

Everyone was there to welcome the new baby.

That first night the parents lay
their baby down to sleep and said,
"Forever and always we will be
your mommy and daddy.
Forever and always you will be
our child."

And they kissed her good night.

Author's Note

In 1991 my husband and I traveled to Central America to meet the baby who was to be our daughter. We spent weeks getting ready, and the feeling of that day was something I wanted to be able to share with Lena when she was older. Having the opportunity to express the magic of adoption with paint and words is a great joy to me. It is my gift to our daughter and to the children and parents who have shared this journey.

Henry Holt and Company, LLC, *Publishers since 1866*
115 West 18th Street, New York, New York 10011

Henry Holt is a registered trademark of Henry Holt and Company, LLC
Copyright © 1997 by Karen Katz. All rights reserved.
Published in Canada by Fitzhenry & Whiteside Ltd.,
195 Allstate Parkway, Markham, Ontario L3R 4T8.

Library of Congress Cataloging-in-Publication Data
Katz, Karen. Over the moon: an adoption story / written and illustrated by Karen Katz.
Summary: A loving couple dream of a baby born far away and
know that this is the baby they have been waiting to adopt.
[1. Adoption—Fiction. 2. Babies—Fiction.] I. Title.
PZ7.K157450v 1997 [E]—dc21 96-37554

ISBN 0-8050-5013-2 (hardcover)
3 5 7 9 10 8 6 4
ISBN 0-8050-6707-8 (paperback)
1 3 5 7 9 10 8 6 4 2
First published in hardcover in 1997 by Henry Holt and Company
First Owlet paperback edition—2001
Designed by Meredith Baldwin
The artist used collage, gouache, and colored pencils to create the illustrations for this book.
Printed in the United States of America on acid-free paper. ∞